She was in a pretty green dress and had golden curls. She was so young, and he wanted to stop, but continued on his way, thinking of how beautiful she was.

One early spring
many years ago,
Zhaawani-noodin,
South Wind, was
very lonely. He was passing
through a field when he saw a
lovely young girl.

"Let me tell you an old Ojibwe story about dandelion," he continued. "It will help you better understand these things." Then he told the story . . .

"I understand," said Father. "It is sad when dandelions leave us to go to the spirit world."

The next morning, Little Dandelion saw that his grandmother was gone. Her brown blossom had fallen to the ground, leaving only her bud. Little Dandelion was sad. He didn't want Bee or Rainwater. He wanted Grandmother.

Little Dandelion squeezed his leaves tight to catch rainwater for Grandmother.

He asked Bee to visit her. That didn't help.

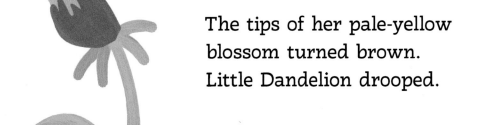

The tips of her pale-yellow blossom turned brown. Little Dandelion drooped.

"She can't," said his mother. "Grandmother is very old. She is going to walk on to the spirit world soon."

One morning, Grandmother stayed in her bud. Her bright yellow florets turned pale. Little Dandelion didn't understand. "Why won't Grandmother come out?" he asked his mother. "There's lots of sun and many bees."

"Grrrr," said
Little Dandelion.

"Grrr," said
Grandmother.

"Why are we called dandelions?" Little Dandelion asked Grandmother one day.

"Because our leaves look like lion's teeth," answered grandmother.

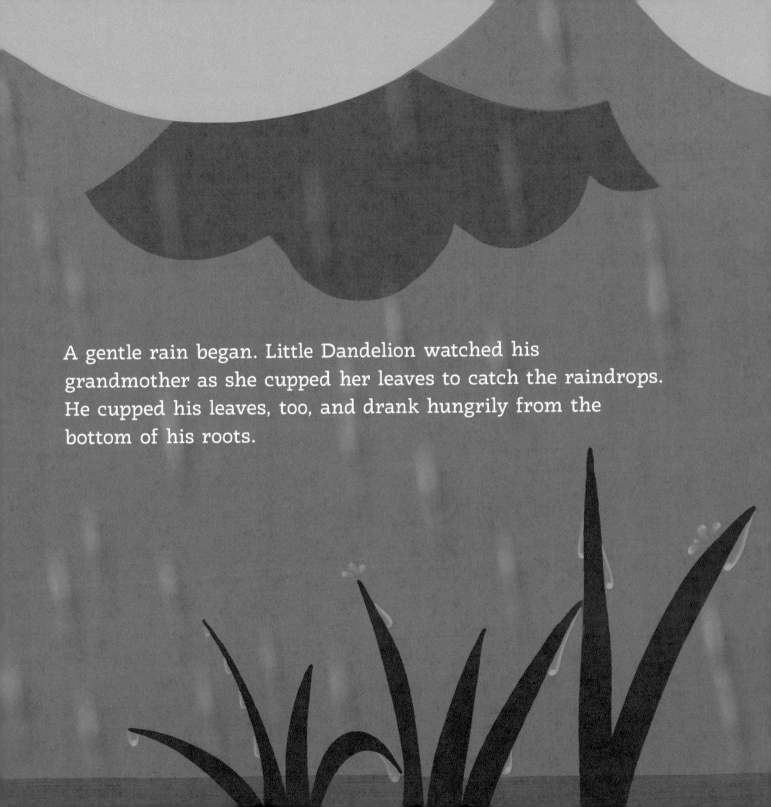

A gentle rain began. Little Dandelion watched his grandmother as she cupped her leaves to catch the raindrops. He cupped his leaves, too, and drank hungrily from the bottom of his roots.

"Don't be afraid," she whispered. Little Dandelion's stalk stood proud. "Not me," he said as he shared his nectar with Bee.

Little Dandelion heard a deafening buzzing sound. A large dark shadow hid the sun. His bottom floret trembled and he looked to his grandmother.

At night, they curled up and cuddled together for a nice, long sleep.

At day's break, they opened and reached for the warm light of the sun.

Finally, he burst out of his bud. He was bright yellow, just like his grandmother, mother, and father. He smiled proudly as he stood high, reaching for the sun.

Little Dandelion pushed against the green covering that held its bright blossom. "Unhhh! Unhhh!" He grunted as he pushed. "Here I come, everybody!"

His mother wrapped her jagged leaves around him. "Come on out, little one," she said.

Little
Dandelion

Written by Rita M. Bergstein and Elizabeth Albert-Peacock
Illustrations by Anna Granholm

The next time he came through, she was even more beautiful. The bees were swarming around her and he knew they needed her nectar, so he passed through again without stopping.

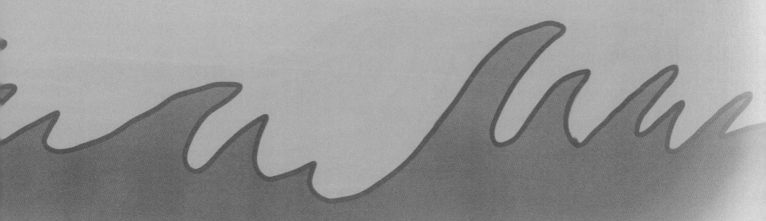

In late summer he
passed through the field
again and saw that her pretty
golden hair was white and green dress was brown. South Wind
had returned to find an old woman.

He realized it was too late. He had put off meeting her
for too long and lost out on love.

He let out a sigh and as he
did the old woman's hair
blew away in the wind and
scattered across the meadow.

The old woman,
Doodooshaboo-jiibak,
Dandelion, cried, for she had
lost all of her beautiful hair.
She was old and lonely. Her
once beautiful dress was
falling around her.

The next day, however, when she looked out on the field there were little flowers with golden heads and they were shining in the sunlight.

She was filled with happiness. "These are my babies, my children," she said. "I once cherished being young and thought all of it was lost when I grew old, but this is the best gift of all. My seeds blew and covered the fields, and one day they too will grow old and cover nimaamaa-aki, mother earth, with beautiful flowers."

"Life to life. The circle of things continues that way," Father said.

A few days later, Little Dandelion watched
in awe at Grandmother's stalk.

From
her bud
erupted a
white, fuzzy ball. The
warm southern breeze caught her
feathers and carried them up, up, up
swirling into the sky. Little Dandelion
smiled. Grandmother lived in the
breeze and sky. Her children would
soon cover the fields.

Little Dandelion welcomed Bee the next time he came to visit. He caught gentle raindrops in his jagged leaves and drank again from his roots. He enjoyed the summer sky and the warm, gentle winds where grandmother went to live.

Glossary

Zhaawani-noodin – south wind
(**zhaawan**/south, **noodin**/wind)

Doodooshaboo-jiibak – dandelion

Nimaamaa-aki – mother earth
(**nimaamaa**/my mother, **aki**/earth)

Dandelion Teachings

The dandelion gives its seeds to the
wind to create a new fresh life. It has learned
to let go, and doing so it continues to nurture the
bees and give us healing medicines. We too must
let go. You will open up to the new gifts life and
spirit has to offer. You can share those gifts as the
dandelion does.

Ojibwe Uses for Dandelions

Young dandelion leaves were used as food and medicine by the
Ojibwe. The roots, flowers, and whole plant were used for back
pain, anemia, liver spots, and sores.

(From Rita) For Mason and Lilliana and any more that may bloom. Grandma loves you.

(From Elizabeth) To my beautiful grandchildren: life isn't about waiting for the storm to pass, it's about learning to dance in the rain. Dance, my Darlings, Dance! Love, Nana

Little Dandelion
© 2023 by Rita M. Bergstein and Elizabeth Albert-Peacock, Illustrations by Anna Granholm

ISBN 978-1-7369493-3-7

Book cover and interior design by Paul Nylander | Illustrada

Black Bears & Blueberries Publishing
www.blackbearsandblueberries.com

A Native owned non-profit publishing company, with a focus on creating and developing Native children's books for all young people written by Native writers and illustrated by Native artists.

Made in the USA
Monee, IL
13 July 2023

38727649R00024